The Loads of poetry

part 2 

Aarchi Advani.!

pencil

ISBN 978-93-5458-190-8
© Aarchi Advani.! 2021
Published in India 2021 by Pencil

A brand of

One Point Six Technologies Pvt. Ltd.
123, Building J2, Shram Seva Premises,
Wadala Truck Terminal, Wadala (E)
Mumbai 400037, Maharashtra, INDIA
E connect@thepencilapp.com
W www.thepencilapp.com

Author biography

Aarchi Advani

[ ] Author of the book "ANJAAN AJNABII", "LIKE FATHER, LIKE DAUGHTER" and "THE LOADS OF POETRY".
[ ] Social media "Aarchi Advani"
[ ] Aries, believe in destiny.

Aarchi Advani is well known for his writing on many other platforms. And overthrowing mankind. She is also a fantasy and literary fiction author specializing in "anjaan ajnabi".
The xoompeace Aarchi Advani also hosts a channel where she uses her passion for storytelling. And a background in business to help other creatives navigate their writing. And publishing journey. When she's not writing or tubing she enjoying listening to books,
Making stories on her own. And love to live in her virtual world.

CONTENTS

The Loads of poetry...

1. Sometimes.

Sometimes there will be talk, sometimes there will be silence,
Sometimes there will be a rain of unanswered questions,
Sometimes there will be Azmayish, sometimes there will be instructions
We will also meet sometime,
Sometimes things will happen, sometimes ...

Every story of my story will have your habits,
My every secret will begin with your name,
Sometimes I will be, sometimes I will be a shadow,
I will have sweet trials every time in your love,
Sometimes things will happen, sometimes ...

I Will never sleep without the burden of desires,
Sometimes only you will have wishes,
Sometimes there will be a life full of food on a plate,
Sometimes a sharp, sweet tip will sparkle,
Sometimes things will happen, sometimes ...

Sometimes love-a-talk will only be with eyes,
You have to understand yourself without ever saying,

My prayer, every prayer will be your name,
Sometimes there will be talk between us, sometimes there
will be silence ...

Aarchi Advani.!

2. Words

You sent an open letter for a poem of our choice
So that you can see the sole and list to the poet's voice
Are you ready and can you handle
Light will sometimes burn a candle
Words will sometimes bind and tangle
To your sole from every angle
Let these words move and creep
And in your heart buried deep
Let these words be eternal
Let them be your book and journal
First I'll say congratulations
448 are proof of patience
45 left good relations
Poets flocked from every nation
Today you witness my invasion
As you read it without evasion
Let it leave you in sensation
Words are jumping in my chest
Locked within a silent vest
Roaring like the wildest beast
Close your eyes and watch them feast
On the vest that won't release
In my eyes, you'll see the storm
See a sea of armies sworn

See Ameen in his form
Only those who can see
Turn around and want to flee
Do not tremble do not fear
You are a poet so your dear.

Aarchi Advani.!

3. Why I love you.?

You are a bright place for me
Who made me think there are thousands of capacities even
if you're unaware

You've made me lovable and it's lovely to be loveable to
the one I love

You've painted my life full of colors more than in your
own canvas.
You didn't take anything from me instead you've left
intense emotions in me.

You've made me believe in uncertainty because at the end
of the day it is memories we cherish not dates.

You've made me notice small beautiful things
You've made me rational and emotional at the same time.

You've made me feel I'm not disappointing.

You've shown me I don't need to stand on a mountain to
feel I'm at the top of the world, but I need someone to

love who will stand beside me.

You've shunned my intuitions beyond what I could've imagined.

I am scared to be ordinary and you are interesting, wanderer, different and that's why I love you.

And in some moments I fear losing hold of your hand.
You know how terrible I feel when I can't be there for you to make you put to in a peaceful sleep.

In the midst of imperfections, you've shown me there is such thing as a perfect day.

I have these feelings as if I am waiting for something, and when I see you I realize it's you.

You are my escape, you are the bright place where I wander. A place with uncountable things to notice and I have all the time in the world to look closely at them.

But One day you left, because you were a bright place not with lights but with fire.

We're burning to brighten up other's lives.
But the difference is I am very close to you and you know when we get close to the fire.

Aarchi Advani.!

4. Mamma

I've tried to write so many times,
But it's been hard to say in rhymes.

I'll try once more and hope you'll see
Just what your love has meant to me.

Thank you for your pain at birth
That brought me to my life on earth.

Thanks for all the time you spent
For cuddles and your nourishment.

Thanks for the parties that you gave
And birthday cards I tried to save.

Thanks for the meals I loved so much
And baking skills that few could touch!

Thanks for the freedom that you gave
To go outside, the world to brave.

Thank you for the friends I'd meet
That helped with friendships I'd repeat.

Thank you for the cures and care
When sickness caught me unaware.

Thanks for tucking me in tight
And kisses on my head instead of saying good night.

When I look at you I see a heart of gold,

Your soul so pure, your love so rich.

Your tender touch so wonderful,
It makes me smile so blissfully.

I could not help, but fall madly in love,
You are the one who stole my heart.

You were strong enough,
Yet gentle enough to be the perfect mother.

You let me know you love me
In so many different ways.

You make me feel important
With encouragement and praise.

Mamma, I wish I had words to tell
How much you mean to me.

I am the person I am today,
Because you let me be.
These words were not adequate to describe you but you
own every piece of me and I love you with my all heart!

Aarchi Advani.!

5. Soul...

You are my favorite song
That can connect to my soul
The more I listen to you

My heart falls and I never knew

I follow every beat of my heart
A pleasing melody in any part
My body dances in your own rhythm
You're like lyrics full of meaning

Your presence is like the brightness of the sun,
The joy of feeling its rays after a cloudy day.
You melt away the cold in me.
And your warmth embraces my whole being.

In the darkness, you are like the moon.
Your light brightens the atmosphere and gives me comfort.
Like the twinkling of the stars,
I can never count the good you have done for me,
Nor can I measures my love for you.

You are like the quiet night,
So peaceful the kid in me comes out to play.
The thought of adventure rushes through my veins.

Like the sunrise
You lose my grumpy face,
And leave me with an undeniable smile.
Like the sunset, that I wish may never pass
You are the moment I just wish to live forever.

You're the light that brought life to the Garden of Eden,
The beating heart of a neutron star.
Gravity to my anti-gravity,

You breathe the cosmos into reality.
Your elegant essence evokes my euphoric entity from oblivion.
The astronomically accurate measurement of the companionship between space, gravity, and time.

You're the sanctuary of my heart,
The archangel who guards my soul,
The neutron that forged my being,
And the andromeda who owns my love.

I found perfection
In every flaw you possessed
In every fault
And every little mistake you did

I found peace
Within your chaos
Tranquility
In your storm
And a passageway
Of love
In heart

Never felt before that
Seven billion hearts beat in unison
When I'm with you.

Aarchi Advani.!

6.A Soul Like You

You are the kind of soul that knows
How to brighten the darkest day
All you gotta do is just say hello
And my frustrations just melt away

You are the kind of soul that is never
Too busy to let me know how you are
All you gotta do is drop me a text message
That lets me know you are never too far

You are the kind of soul that
Tells me the right words to stay encouraged
All you gotta do is say the tough times
Drift away when I refuse to remain discouraged
You are the kind of soul that can make me
Laugh when I really need a much-needed break
All you gotta do is just remain strong
When all I wanna do is just escape

You are the kind of soul that knows
How to keep me grounded without losing control
All you gotta do is free me from confusion
So I know God will never let me go

You are the kind of soul that can
Tell when something is not quite right.

Aarchi Advani.!

7. we're neath the same sky

thee a clocking storm,

hurricane I can naught pass
catastrophic ruinous breath
I inhale
quadruple syllable
 buried in a deep prison
of pallet skin savoring
my crest
eventide to bones
burgundy exodus spill

odious paradox to mine
weaved galaxy
slave of ejection
yet manifest affirmation
with every atom thee plucked
from me
grind my torso into
interstellar dust within thy
 galatic vapors cluster fog
from supernova
nebulas
mummified within
pandora receptacles
arduously poisoning ever
mapping mine trial towards
aftermaths
blinded
in murky maddening amour
still pirouetting underneath
drenching cardinal
ache

drab
all essence of thee
 like champagne stained stein
brooding weigh over me
  diary of corneum gazebo
dipped in grievance
grid
when words
seal lips muting rims
killing me inside carving more
craving whispers
begging to absolve
in the castle of
Aerus
terrified, ashtray
unbloomed, capsulated
within dark seashell
I ponder myself
either way withering darkly lit
breathing dead, intruder lie
 is satiating poppy seed
digging grave six-inch abysmic
with unmown linen
thus...
we're neath the same sky

" I don't know what's killing me more,
talking to you or not talking to you"

Aarchi Advani.!

8. I'D CHOOSE YOU AGAIN AND AGAIN…..

MISTY WAS THE MORNING OF LATE JANUARY,

IN THOSE CUPS OF COFFEE, WERE YOUR ENDURING MEMORY….

SOUNDS OF THE SIPS TOOK ME THOSE BREATHTAKING KISSES,

SIGHS OF BREATH GAVE ME THE SMELL OF YOUR TRACES…..

YOUR HALF BITTEN CHOCOLATES HAD AN ESSENCE OF YOUR LIPS,

OUR DREAM WAS MORE THAN THOSE FANTASIZED SHIPS….

UNDERHEARD WAS MY STORY WITH ITS ANGULAR AND SHAKY SCRIPTS…

QUIVERED BY MY FRIEND I CAME BACK TO MY SENSES,

UTTERING WORDS OF NUISANCE, AS HIS PUNCH WAS INTENSE….

"EXCRUCIATING WAS HER ABANDONMENT", I CRIED,

"EVERLASTING WILL NOT BE YOUR PAIN", HE REPLIED…..

NEVERTHELESS, I BELIEVED THAT I SHALL BE WRETCHED,

AUSPICIOUS WAS SHE IN THOSE PUFFS OF HALF-BURNT CIGARETTES….

LOVE DOESN'T LOVE ME AND IT'S HARD TO FORGET.

Aarchi Advani.!

9. You're a part of me...

The way each motif adds a little bit of essence
To the mosaic.

Even if you're a broken glass the mirror
Every piece of you
Opens up and reflecting you as a fragile work of art, ended
up in despair.
They lost their thoughts
Like a lustrous prism in a mythical dream
By seeing every angle of yours
That is twisted in forms
A new magnificent presence.

You're the man that I dearly admire
And I forever will be fascinated by
How steadfast you are.

Darling, you were already bewitching.
You were born from the sky,
A divine demonstration of mortal virtue.
There is no beauty in your pain,
There is merely pain amongst your beauty
I am not overwhelmed
but I am stunned by your beauty.

You assist me opened up to me
You redesigned my thoughts.
Your paintbrush stroked
Albright blush onto my cheeks
You turned me into
Bright kaleidoscope
With heavenly light
Overwhelming scarlets
And masquerade lilies.

Every emotion,
Dressed me with rainbows,
And completed my blank spaces.
You turned me into a mosaic
But before you could sign your
Glorious artwork
And I realized
I could do better pieces
And masterpiece was overrated anyways.

You and I under the same rainbow,
All of a sudden the displeasures
From the day before slowly
Melt away into the dark nighttime.

In the syzygy of our cosmic hearts
We bask in the ethereal glow encompassed
Comfortably by the sky and stars.
Involved in a state of a constant
Somnambulism so I never have left
The blissful reality conceived in my subconscious.

And I will place you with mine and
We will be immortalized in mosaic.

Flowers and kisses are beautifully tragic
But I'd rather give you your constellation in
A bundle of soft clouds
And a gentle warm breeze
Scented with chamomile and oak pines.

Aarchi Advani.!

10. That raw round-
It was like a rough round,
Strong on one side and
From the other side, it was absolutely raw.
Even though both ways,
The relationship was not sure.

It was just a walk like a raw phase,
Was incomplete, or had never been made
It was just a meeting,
Nothing more than that
Things were incomplete
But things never started.

It was a half-story like a raw phase,
As it was,
It was very beautiful,
Was incomplete,
But it was complete in itself.

The story was not a story,
Not too big
Just some words story was incomplete.

Aarchi Advani.!

11. A word...

Confined in an alphabet
It was the light of the stars,
It goes away,
This was just the beginning of this story.

Confined in an alphabet,
It was the light of the stars,
There was not much time,
Nevertheless, this story was as if the story was a story.
It was the end, but the beginning was complete.
Confined in an alphabet,
It was like starlight.

As if everything was being snatched away,
Everything was going away,
Just by leaving him,
The new beginning was also the end.

Confined in an alphabet,
It was like starlight,
Yes, it's not like the end,
That was the end of me and I was the beginning of me.

Aarchi Advani.!

12. In the darken dungeon;

In the darken dungeon;
after midnight crystalline focused
down into susceptible anacondas
withing screaming dangerous waters

the memory of a dreaming
leading me by myself into hands
falling into hollows hole grounded rounded
with your arms of strong syringing sweat
are what I finding love to endured founded

the moonlights each night our faces
that loneliness eyes;
with her lures tenderness moments awaiting
within her beautiful shape eyes of blues
like a coyote out in the wild to singing

longing again to seeking love
to fall down to face marriage
that deepest, deeper 'n deeply
that leads me intoxicated nightstands ~
back tomorrow's lovingly most misty shadows.

Aarchi Advani.!

13. I am yours until the.

I am your's until the world apart from us.
I am your's until nature apart us.
I am your's until the country apart us.
I am your's until the state apart us.
I am your's until the district apart us.
I am your's until the society apart us.
I am your's until the casteism apart us.
I am your's until the universe apart from us.
I am your's until anyone can apart us.
Don't read after until.
I will always your's.
Even after all this.
Even after apart from each other, I am yours.

Aarchi Advani.!

14. Same.

We are lying under the same universe.
we are flying in the same sky.
we are walking on the same ground.
we are smiling for the same reasons.
we're crying for the same sadness.
we are living on the same planet.
we are using the same water, air, electricity.
then what makes us different, if you are counting what

makes us different than even the zero will also not support
you.

Aarchi Advani.!

15. the ballad of bochephus

bocephus blew his nose
and his huge bulbous head exploded
in front of women and children
leaving many wearing a grin

the gross mohair toupee
that was growing out his ears
landed in a babies buggy
on his baby snuggly

bereft of eloquent words
to speak over his grave
to say nothing of him
is more than I will say

to begin with
the end has come
oddly he has nothing to say
once indulgences they pay

less than nothin
is what they had today
laid to rest with his sock puppet
and his three-piece pink hair net.

Aarchi Advani.!

16. Darlin

Darlin, I don't want to be remembered
When I turn into ash and dust
I wanted to be remembered
When my bones were alive
But you failed to show.

So that when the flames
Of my life blown out,
I'll be able to enter
Death peacefully
Knowing that I'm a selfless lover
But a fool for sure.

I shall try, very hard,
not to be afraid
when black night falls.
For I have always been afraid
of that which creeps and calls
through unilluminated hours.

There was solace in the darkness
Before I opened myself to you.

I'm a paper skin and fragile bones
Only flesh, in the end, makes
Its bed in the brown grass.

The layer beneath all layers,
on which everything rests,
is built,
grows,
thrives
then dies.
I'll be returned again to the lower layers
where it can take root again
and grow out onto the great plains.

Aarchi Advani.!

17. Maybe

Maybe I'll find it was just one shade I've been chasing all along.

I've grown a little darker these days. Or maybe I've just been in the
shadow so long it's hard to tell which shade I am.
When I was a kid, my little fingers always had this fascination with
those pretty pink shades. Always wondering how clouds would look like
cotton candy if pink. Those moments don't come back, do they?
When I grew a little older, the rainbow was the most fascinating thing I'd
come across. No combinations, no contrast. Just a few random shades put
together, becoming one of the most beautiful makings of

nature.
When I reached a stage where nights seemed calmer, I started caressing
the darker hues, filling my voids with blacks and greys. Gazing up at the
sky, I wanted nothing more than to become a part of it.
But now, all I see is how the paint splashes all over the sky, when the sun
sets and how I wish I could put it into words. Or how the clouds land on
earth just for a moment and how I keep wishing to escape with them. Or
how from loving one shade, I've stained the canvas in so many colors
that I have lost my hue among them.
And when the time comes, maybe I'll find it was just one shade I've been
chasing all along.

Aarchi Advani.!

18. Questions

What do I write about my sadness now when every word I
wrote turned into another dying world that nobody cared
about as long as they were safe. What do I say and how
do I say that it hurts too much? Sometimes this sadness
crashes like a wave on the shore of my body and I feel like
the ground beneath my feet moved a little. And on other
days, it's sO still that no amount of tragedy can nudge it
into action. I am not a writer who can wake you up from
your inertial indifference. All am asking for is help. I am

exhausted from all these sympathetic friendships which
never turn around to see if l am even here. I know people
don't need me now. I am as alive as I am dead. And my
death won't even induce a reaction amidst people when all
they would say is that they knew, after all it was obvious.
But

you don't tell a dying man that death awaits him: you ask
for what he wishes for. I don't even wish for life anymore.
wish for peace. In those last moments, I wish for regret in
the eyes of people who thought that I was a failed case
of an MD resident who couldn't include me in his final
thesis of degree well because I didn't behave in a way test
subjects should behave. I wish for revenge. For reducing
me into a file name when I was an individual all this while
with a disease that was just a part of me and not my entire
self. I wish to pass this hell from me to those who thought
I was just another person who couldn't manage life and
bowed down instead to pray for mercy. This may seem
sadistic but I am too tired to be alive. And when I say I
need

peace, I don't mean death but a pause. From living. lying.
surviving and suffering. And if this is too much to ask for,
I

don't know if at this point I am the one at fault, or you are,
who is witnessing a decay right in front of your eyes and
calling it a process. This is not a process. This is the end
of a beginning. And I can't scream anymore. I can't. So l
let

my silence be the weighing burden on your shoulders just
so when you ask where it went wrong. you don't know the
answers. I hope you never find one.

Aarchi Advani.!

19. Help

When the world around is silent
Do you even make noise to let them know that
you are still here
This deafening loneliness that curses me
A voodoo doll of infñinite misery
Wonder if it is praise when someone says that I am
too silent nowadays
Isn't the world too?
I look for hope
One more reason to continue
When everyday life speaks mundane depression
That carries me like a child
And I sleep on its lap for escape
The lake at a distance from my home
Is so still
No ripples of time or sun wake it up
From its utter meditation

It is still like blue and death
Green and spring
Yellow and summer afternoon
I can't help but think about walking on water
I mean someone has to take the baton to jolt the world
back into its hustle-bustle.
But who will?
can't wake up

And neither does God
Where are all the prayers disappearing?
In these four walls of the home
I feel as if they watch me
My room no more a room
But a stage and these lifeless ceiling. walls, a noisy cooler
My spectators
I dance for them sometimes
And play dress up the others
But nothing about this room Screams home
Nothing about this world screams home
We indeed were made to be lonely
Or how else can you explain the distance between atoms
Their interaction, a lover's touch
Their separation, an annihilation
So tell me where to go
if not on an adventure that asks me to Jump off a cliff
Without blinking my eyes
And call it a destiny
A messed up fate
A dead man's wings
A living man's attempt at dying
--- I want to be at home, I am tired of screaming for help.

Aarchi Advani.!

20.A Beautiful Daze

The gradual opening of the curtains and blinds,
letting in the enticing shine.
Through the pupilled window and wired maze,

projection of the beautiful daze.

Swiftly reaching the unscathed heart,
opening up the guarded cage.
Skillfully stealing glimpses and stares,
the brightest beam upon the rosy face.

Aarchi Advani.!

21. Everything...
Everything around us has a story,
Everything around us has words to tell.
Everything around us inspires you, to write.
Everything around us, teaches you, that nothing is impossible.
Everything around us helps you in every way that can.
Everything around us.
Remember, Everything around us.

Aarchi Advani.!

22. Lie

The Thing that connects us, In real wasn't for us.
In the love we are living in, that love wasn't for us.
The care they are giving us wasn't for us.
Those words that made us feel special, aren't written for us.
The life we are living doesn't belong to us.
Even the one for whom we think, that the one we are always here for us,
That one was lost very before from us.

We are living a life.
We are living a lie.

Aarchi Advani.!

23. Spark

That spark on her face, I will never gonna erase.
That smile on her lips, will never gonna ditch.
Love, sorrow, care or her smile,
Fades everything of others,
when we are talking about her.

Everything seems faded,
Like we see roses with their thorn.
Like lotus in mud.
The spark on her face, I will never gonna erase.

Staying happy with reason is your option.
But keep smiling even without reason is her only desire.

Aarchi Advani.!

24. Fly

Like air, I want to fly.
Flying everywhere.
There is just a feeling of presence.
I want to live a life, not a lie tho.

Aarchi Advani.!

25. Silence...

Silence has many answers,
But you are full of noise.
Silence can give you the solution to even those problems,
which have no solution.
But you think you are enjoying your life.
Silence always stands back foot,
Like your backbone always.
But you never look back, you never keep silent in your
anger.

Silence is the best teacher and you think you can teach
yourself on your own.
This silence is no one, but your inner voice peace.
Just give it a try.

Aarchi Advani.!

26. Numb...
Before I tried to make myself numb.
But seeing you sad make me sad;
Seeing you hurt make me worried;
As long as I saw you happy and smiling,
I would feel content.
It was then that I realized, I couldn't lie to myself.
That I have feelings for you.
That I care more about you than myself.
I think more about you than myself.
I live in you more than myself.

you are more inside me than myself.

Aarchi Advani.!

27. Heartache...
Have you ever met someone, and felt your heartache.?
Have you ever thought of someone and suddenly feel like crying.?
Ask yourself why?
why is it so unbearable.?
Is it because you care for him.?
or there is something else.?
Just ask why?

Aarchi Advani.!

28. Earlier

I just realized that, If there's the moon;
There are no stars.
If there are stars,
There's no moon.
But life changes;
Look that golden star is still bright.
It's just its position that hid it.
There is just a point of view of seeing something.

Aarchi Advani.!

29. Jumper Cables (Song)

Growing faded in my daze
Caked and coated haze
Gone in my head, two weeks
I'm so weak in my knees
My heart is cold to the touch
This life bears way too much
She was the 'shine in my cup
I once was to hold her up
Ever since you left like that
I told you to go, **** that

I need a jumper cable for my heart
To my heart
I feel so unstable, I'm falling apart
It's my fault
I need a jolt of life, I'm dying light
Dying light
I feel so unstable, I'm falling apart
It's my fault
Nothing left within my room.

Aarchi Advani.!

30. [Left foot, right foot, mouth on mute,]

Left foot, right foot, mouth on mute,
Left-click, right-click, do not think,
Left Sir, Right Sir, may I diverge?

Have you tried to catch a feather,
With nothing but forcing the nether,

Moving the air, derailing the tether,
Reality being farther than ever,
For we cannot conquer but we can sever.

These lines that cross my mind,
Are waiting to be cracked wide,
Opening a core with no games, no lies,
These small walls cannot hide hides,
Especially when the leather is mine.

This smell, permeating every interaction,
Foul, rotten, a devil's prized creation,
Soft, sweet acidic tinge in intonation.

It's my choice, my own direction,
The last of my own rebellions,
A right to ignore recommendations,
'Cause you all leading into empty sections,
When my heart is demanding attention.

Standing too close to the cliff,
Nostrils inundated with mundane whiffs,
Teetering with two feet over the edge,
Holding myself with only a sense of dread,
That I will not smile when my body smashes into the end.

I want to smile when I die,
To be proud of what's lost,
My greatest fear is not paying the cost,
Of not laying my soul to what's just,
To be simply in history, another regular page.

Aarchi Advani.!

31. 'Personal Exploration'

At this moment and forevermore
I am broken, straight to the core.
I think of what my future has in store,
But first, a new me I must explore.

Daunting is the things hidden in the deep,
With hope and faith in hand, I choose to leap.
The outcome of my thoughts and actions I reap,
And dreams of past, present, and future plague my sleep.

I search but not in stealth
As I explore my newfound self.
I pray to find an inner wealth
That deals with life and personal health.

Aarchi Advani.!

32. I Can't Be Stopped!

(written as character Majeek Dawson)

The Cabal is in grave danger
Their desperation has put Majeek Dawson
In bed with his anger
Attempting to shut me down
Orchestrating unnecessary distances

Between strangers,
Kinfolks and friends alike
The unseen leader is about
To go take an ill-fated hike
Out into the deadliest depths
Of the woods...I could...I should...
I would...NO! **** THAT! I AM!
The deal has already been sealed
Soldiers on the astral plane
Are moving in for the kill
Blasting on The Cabal
Deleting or white-outing their wicked plot
My kitchen is no ****en place to be
When it gets this hot
They might as well gracefully bow out
Because I can't be stopped!
There's no such possibility
I can't be stopped!
The Cabal is in grave danger
Their desperation has put Majeek Dawson
In bed with his anger
Getting rid of the bullshit distances
Between strangers,
Kinfolks and friends alike
The unseen leader is too afraid
To step up to me on a public mic

Majeek speaking on the 'powers that be' and his plans to ruffle their feathers.

Aarchi Advani.!

33. Artist.

They say love is
the driving force of the artist.
The words that spill upon
the page is inspired by
the butterflies in their belly.
The stars in their eyes are caused by
a glance at their lover
that must be the reason
why my pages are empty
and it matches the contents of my heart.

How could someone be so perfect
With all the imperfectness you have
I never believed the word perfect
Until you with all your cracks,
stood in all your glory.

I desperately want to fold myself
in your poem because
they're a scent of withering
flower of love and
the only language of lost love and
pain.

I want to burn myself and
make something of the ash.
I feel like a great
almost completed puzzle

expansive and vast
dull pieces
but still connected
now one-piece has been
taken from me and
has been replaced
replaced by a misshapen mess
in the guise of a puzzle piece
and as I desperately try to shove
it in its previous spot
I scream and push my hands
across the table
disconnecting the pieces
in my plight.

How smooth I would become!
worn to my bones
by ceaseless motion,
wearing the patina of eternity.
I would sigh upon the mud
settling into a shape of my own lotus.

In my heart, I know
seeds of
my lotus is just a fossil
same as all the rest,
who lie in wait
to be picked over —
anticipating selection
or discarded.
I'll bloom on death
when I'm feeling down

so I can cry to something new.

I watch a life burn
down to dusty ash
from a tiny,
yellow gas flame
That lights the cigarette
in his hand
That churns out words
from his troubled brain.

A writer's violence hides,
not in his eyes,
But in angry,
quivering palms that trace
A venomous, untidy, familiar scrawl
Reducing their complexity
to scribbles on a page.

Aarchi Advani.!

34. Moon and stars.

I wish I could commit the moon and stars,
But alas the world is too
Realistic and practical for me.
There is much that holds me back
Cause of the baggage
I have to carry out my past.
My world had dreams, fantasies, love, craziness
And all those aspects that are supposed to be
Enjoyed but forbidden.

There is much about you to remember
Am terrified I might forget
To me appears you already have
The realization that makes me upset.

Nothing to stop the image from fading
From brain a bit more each day
Picture your face so clearly now
Know time will steal it away

Many times I wondered,
How you come back to this land
Where the scary hand of the butcher
Scuttles every dream;
Where humanity drowns
In its own anguished cries
Just to see my smile while gazing
Dead infinite stones engraved upon skies.

The smell of blood is
Intoxicating when its grasp
Tightens like a noose
On my consciousness.

You told me once that
Writing all our memories
The best way to ensure
In some way, I'll preserve you forever
The perfect specimens we were
If I could have one wish

I wish we would be hanging on forever but
Fate set fire to our map.

But darling, words are meaningless
and forgettable feelings are fleeting
and unreliable presents get old and
Worn out.
People change
from friends to strangers and
Change is inevitable.
Nothing remains the same even
this paper town lead my feelings
Down various times.

Without you, the sun will strip away my skin,
And my blood is braided in an unknown identity.

I wish I could tell you that sometimes
Your eyes are like planets,
wide and round with wonder and
A beautiful love song with muted
Words for God's silent melodious prayer.
They speak beauty and
Ameliorate mess of my heart and
I became infected by intoxicating eyes every time.

Brown shiny hairs as James Dean
that stay stuck in memory
melting me like hot cocoa
and reminds me of home
those who hook with yours
one more time and forever.

So, I'm freezing precious snapshots of yours
Because to you, they did not matter
If love was a delicate vase
You would purposefully topple it
Simply to see shatter.

Aarchi Advani.!

35. Darkness

I've been told once before
that when you stare into the Darkness
it begins to stare back at you

Until I visited
your grave
I never believed them.

I sat and stared
at the nameless headstone
callously placed amongst the shadows
and I mourned

My tears falling delicately
on the loose soil that concealed
what was left of you?

Until I held your hollow lifeless skull
in my trembling fragile hands
and met your tender gaze.

I cry on the behalf of those people
who alienated you till this day.

Even someone without flesh and
organs shouldn't look so empty inside
like me on this day.

The warm dirt hug you more than anyone
else ever did in your entire existence.

You never make a sound
Yet your sadness echoes deafeningly.

Do your bones not feel cold out in the dark?
Does not being able to shed tears make
Are you unable to release your sadness?

Poor little me, won't know what else to do!
but tear into themselves,
crying for all of eternity
but they say that tragedy is a beauty,
which is why the flowers blossom
over your pitiful grave.
Laughable almost,
to be the source of your own misery.

Why do you still look so sad?
Things that killed you, it's over now.

And my love of is six feet under with

his beloved in eternal glory.

I hope you don't think that
your existence was a tragedy
Though in the end I never managed
to make you alive even once.

As you've told them to bury
you next to her grave
But I promise you that
I'll always stand by your grave until
the fighting flame of my life goes off.

How funny, person whose life was crowned
with cactus of fake love now lying
beneath the scented nature blooming
upon his grave with his stone cold-hearted lover like
pedestrian she also alienated, displaced, and destroyed you
every nanosecond.
Wasted her life studying what made
Van Gogh to suicide and bombarded his heart
with lies and the art of disappearing.

Aarchi Advani.!

36. Words...

Your words are like fine melancholic metaphors
I'll love to taste them slowly
Unleashing each syllable in your chaotic mind
Not all poems have to rhyme
But some of your writings are a crime.

Your words reveal the hidden mysteries of the earth
And wrists bleed pure misery like
they never glanced at love
Let your pain be a river pouring joy;
and flood the ravenous world.

An assault against art and words that wield power
This effort attempts to resonate
hundred times each hour
I bet Sylvia Plath turns in her grave
At these pathetic bids, some of you gave
Creating dense prose that contains the line
Every night, brand new lacuna of life
you start to define.

People are patterns,
and all you knew was
the fleeting framework of love and
permanent loss.

//He couldn't be more than twenty-five,
but he obviously lived enough
to have things to regret.
He looked like he'd taken
a long fall a short time ago.
Pieces of the man he'd been
were jumbled up with the new guy,
the lost soul.//

Your syllables are a bird
It flies over great seas of time

Of things I've never heard;
I may ever watch it fly divinely
Your wrists bleed pure misery like
they never glanced at contentment
And I'm not the first and surely not
the last one to admire them.

You're a colorful courageous chocolate cosmos
A charming consummate nettle
that you may come across once in your lifetime.

Your love is as delicate
As a butterfly cleansing its wings
As soft as the predicate of hummingbird
Sings to itself as a gentle murmuring.

I want you to like the light of twinkling dots,
Because the dimness of your presence
Doesn't always end up disappearing.

It's the silence of the night that makes
your thoughts so loud
Mist of memories encompasses your mind
Thoughts of yesterdays yearn to be felt and
carved out.

Aarchi Advani.!

37. Medicine Taken Daily

He had been there

There where viciousness had revealed itself
A blank expression now lay on his face
Lots of time to reflect

There is no escape
No unplugging from what he had done
The beast residing within is his
And he's alone.

Aarchi Advani.!

38. Back Alley Paul

they can bust my balls cuz I didn't spit-it with
Crystal Geyser at the flames the lines I wrote came with
and I'll stand tall
like-a back alley Paul takin' his lumps jumped by
nothin but-a-bunch-uh crooks
out of-a ride
with more bumps than-a 1st case of chickenpox.

but what they can't do
is say
that I wasn't an original recipe
bawk—bawk-bawk
Written in response
to my blog being temporarily shut down
No biggie - fixed.

Aarchi Advani.!

39. your power

my first listen
a Billie Eilish track
your power

and that I felt

taken
her charm suffers no loss
stems of grain leaps out the dark
covets his hold reels her in
passed the cut
a line not drawn crows press that shapes me
I know how it rests
given you a trip and trace.

Aarchi Advani.!

40. All is well...

All you gotta do is ask if all is well and
If I can remain strong through my hardest nights

You are the kind of soul that has
A special way of taking the right kind of action
All you gotta do is smile at me and

Let me know all I need is a diversion from difficult
reactions

You are the kind of soul that
Is always faithful to the heart
All you gotta do is just be there and
I feel at peace right from the start

You are the kind of soul that knows
When it's time to laugh or time to mend broken fences
All you gotta do is just help me
Not become a victim of helpless circumstances

You are the kind of soul that I can
Count on through every season of life
All you gotta do is just be true to me
When my goodness is overcome by relentless strife

You are the kind of soul everyone
Wishes he or she had for a trusted friend
All you gotta do is just be therewith
A special spirit that remains faithful to the end.

Aarchi Advani.!

41. Thalassophile......

Roaming hands
On beach sand,
Soft and delight.

The sunset was melting in waves,
So I was melting
I thought of the love of mine.

Rhythms of waves...
Rise and ebbs.
So my heart does...
Thoughts of love.
Hold my breath...
Sun is just going to kiss the sea,
Horizon has all bliss.

Slowly the waves ;
Are whispering with the sky.
So does the wind with sand,
Tinted paperwork with shells,
Is the glory of divine...

White creamy waves,
Touching the feet of mine,
Feels the starlight sparkling,
My bones in the twilight.

Salty smell,
Of wind
&
flora around.
Has a heart of sea canvas rocks.

I'm lost with words,

Every time I hear the melody of waves,
Screaming in my eardrums,
'You have to sink in or
Settle,
Every drop of pain
Will be consumed in me..'
I'm in love with those words of the melody
Cause it's always calm.
To the heart of a person like me (Thalassophile).

Aarchi Advani.!

42. I find no one here, can I speak today, please?

"Listen, can we talk? If you don't mind."
No, I won't mind, you know what keeping things under
the lantern has burned me completely. I won't say those
things were mistakes for me. But better I will say those
things moulded me stronger and different from what I
was. I won't mind saying that I have been waiting for
hours to smile and stop with fear that what if someone
notices me. I won't mind today saying I can't love anyone
because everything ended that day itself when I was
wondering what's further?.
I won't mind saying I was weak to point out who am I. I
won't mind today bursting out in tears in front of you
because I know no more fit in the frame of your space. I
won't mind telling you today I had lost everything in
between, even myself, I can't see anyone say out things,
My heart has been more of a burden, I can't believe but

attached everything changed. I won't mind telling you today, after you, I didn't found any person saying me stop crying and hugged me as
if I'm small kid craving affection.
I won't mind telling you today, I'm trying to forget your patches on my childhood, teenage and might be today in youth.
Will you mind me saying this out today?

Aarchi Advani.!

43. Love...

Bird once loved me.
: Is no longer mine.
Let it go.
Let it explore the world.
t never believed in existence in my galaxy.
It belonged to another galaxy.
Let it find saféty in other's roots.
Let it share the stories of its high flights with new ones.
Let it be happy with new ones.
Let its laughter be appreciated by new ones
who can't stop the bird. Just l can pray for me.
bird.. which was never mine...

Aarchi Advani.!

44. New Learner of life.

Friday
4:30A.M
28th May

New Learner of life.....
Beginning of learning...Oh my god!!! It was damn difficult...
It was the unpredictable deportment of life that leads to a confusing freeze to my imperfections.
Harder, I tried to come out; deeper I was getting involved...
Scattered nights with thousands of emotions and thoughts. And worthless days with no paths of love...
As I was a new learner, I was curiously wondering to know every single thing... How to get out of this sad moment of mine?
Yeah...But I must say it gave me a view that life is beyond ideas of wrongdoing and right doing...
Learning of life gave my dreams of novel love a tight slap & took me to the saddest reality...
I was wondering in myself,'...Is the universe trying to break me from all ends?'... but somehow I learned, it takes courage to heal yourself.
The idea of constant stay of anyone in our life is
a fake idea.
Some chapters of life are bad. Sorry. I must say their endings are bad. But the courage to move on with new hope is telling of the universe that you have more and more than you have already planned...And hopefully, it can be bliss to your paths...

Afraid of loved ones leaving scares ...it still scares me. I still don't know how to get out of this mess???
But then too as a good learner; now I learned not to break the spark of inner strength again and again; for one who no longer deserves me...
My opened eyes have new but bad experiences...
But

Somehow my professor (Life) taught me to enjoy my journey for my own pleasure, to recognize my existence for the journey, taught me not to run from my mistake, decisions, past but to tackle the situation for the betterment of myself.
Gave me the capacity to think I'm enough to heal my scars rather than to keep one good healer.

Ohh!! I know I'm not a good learner of life but I try to keep my lesson alive ♡♡
Aarchi Advani.!

45. I'm a girl

Yes,
    I'm a girl
           And
                I don't like pink

I know
It's hard to decode my rhymes
I know
It's hard to understand me sometimes

Sometimes
You won't find my heart's link
Yes,
        I'm a girl
                    And
                        I don't like pink

I like to fly free
And wanna grow freely like a tree
But my wings shrink
When you stare at me without any blink
Yes,
        I'm a girl
                    And
                        I don't like pink

You know what
Just remember that
I'm fed up of this desperately that I see
I mind my business and
you too... just sip your tea
Bczz this nature of yours is just a stinky clink
Yes,
        I'm a girl
                    And
                        I don't like pink

Lemme feel proud of being a girl
Not a fear
Lemme do what I want
Without any tear
Because...

Yes,
     I'm a girl
               And
                    I don't like pink
Yes,
     I'm a girl
               And
                    If I'm alone, my boat won't sink.

Aarchi Advani.!

46. Life.
When life gives you lemons
When you're all around demons
Who is trying to make you depressed
Who's presence is making you stressed
Just peep into yourself and hear the inner voice
Which says...
You are strong!
You are brave!!
You are courteous!!!
You are the diamond in the star
Believe me,
You are the brightest which I met so far
So don't struggle with the people around you
Just be yourself and feel the positivity that surrounds you.

Aarchi Advani.!

47. Her Name

Fire is her lip
lures and licks prey
the black widow is her name
river writhes with blood
rose is her weapon
a lonely queen
lingers in the dark
counting trophies
corpses in torrent
They teach her
Kill and Scars
and dye her eyes
with dead bubbles
Training, a sweet lover
she flirts with salivating monsters
But when empty nights
suck her skin, beetles climb
the cold, dry moonlights
dust swirling in the agency
She still waits to kiss
within closing eyes
In gunpowder
decayed cologne.

Aarchi Advani.!

48. Demon and Angel's.

The moist air and bright green grass joined the stone and
tears to make the saddest smell of time. There you see a
weathered stone forest of forgotten names of broken

people in a broken frame. Great furnace of flame bleak no light but visible darkness. It only serves to discover the sight of angels and demons who are tied and died together.

The words on those introductory stones connect you with me by succeeding vignettes and give significance to the rock standing up alone in a dead sea like the two ships becalmed on torpid turquoise sea and believed to capsize in the marine reservoir of treasure and wonder. As same as the novel's dilemma ends breathtakingly beautiful and bewitch the human race.

Of these dead white realms I formed an idea of my own shadowy existence like the half comprehended notions that float dim through young's mind, but strangely impressive.

In the beginning, how the heaven rose out from chaos and delight each soul like brimming Braden brook that flowed and followed by the angels. Invoke the aid to my brood heart to sail high in blue velvet abyss with my mighty wings outspread to soar above the Andes mount. I've got one last wish on my bucket list is to live for the destination with or without a mortal framework. I bow my head down to space who measures day and night 365 times with his horrifying crew.

Soul resisted between the crystal vast sky and billowing turquoise sea. Gazing cold and ghastly newly-risen crescent moon glancing, attesting the hours of eventide of life through bars of cloud at a wrench before sinking. I was slowly but surely deteriorating and fading away. I was just somebody's escape and maybe the protagonist they only needed.

Each grave tells a tale, mysterious often to my undeveloped understanding and imperfect feelings, yet ever glamorously interesting. As interesting as the tale of Hardy narrated on the lonely evening of winter, fed our eager attention with passages of love and despair taken from mythical fairy tales and other epics. I was happy at least in my way with my muse. I feared nothing but interruption and that fled to me very soon.

Aarchi Advani.!

49. Miracle...

It was a miracle you chose me and
a blessing I took for granted too often.
Maybe I knew I didn't deserve
such an angel so
I pushed you away in hopes
you'd fly to better things.

If you find happiness someplace
far from me
I beg you to stay there.
Because with my own
shattered pieces I hurt those
I love and the more that
I care the deeper I cut.

When I see you lying lifeless there
fighting for one more breath
I catch my own and shed a tear
for the body dying.
You turn your stare away from
death to face me instead
as your eyes are immediately
flooded with fear.

It's not till that moment I realize what
I have done to the only person who
meant more to me
than anything or anyone.
I swear I just wanted to keep you safe and
I thought you were safer away from me
but somehow you got too close again
without me realizing.

Practically under my skin but before
I could see I ripped you to shreds
unaware of who I was destroying in my haste.
But what scraps were left there
I immediately recognized though
your features were all out of place.

Now there is not enough of you to put
your parts back together and we both know
you can live half a human forever.
I hate myself for digging a grave too busy
to notice you return to me in my desperate state.

It's the silence of the night that makes

the thoughts of you so loud
I warned you but too late you learn and
now not just myself but both of us are
far too gone to save.

Aarchi Advani.!

50. tw-self harm

In tenth grade, I began to notice the struggle and tension between my outer and inner self. To most people, I had everything I could want. My family was blessed, my friends were caring, and I had no real worries. Yet, on the inside, I was hopeless, lonely, and cold. Looking in the mirror, I saw a lifeless, unrecognizable human. Unrecognizable. Two different selves fighting to win. One was lucky: wealthy and loved. One was depressed: lonely and suicidal. So I searched.

I searched for ways these two different identities could match. And that? That is self-sabotage. I set myself on fire- -ruining my relationships, isolating myself. Maybe then, my emotions would be justified. Maybe then, people would realize the magnitude of my pain. Maybe then, I could get help.
The silver blade lays, untouched, in your bathroom. You grab it, just to see how it feels. It's sharp, you notice, as you carefully lay it in your hand. That night, you felt really depressed. Yet, all your parents know is that you went out to a party. They have no idea how much you are fighting with yourself, wanting to die, to end it all. One little slice,

just one, for the anxiety attack you had an hour ago. Another one for going home early. One more, only one more, I promise, for that ache inside.

Finally, finally, you see your inner emotions reflected on your outside. For the first time, they match. That fire, that fire that I once lit to burn myself, was finally entering the outside world. But it kept burning. It couldn't stop. Once my parents felt the heat, I realized it was burning them too. I only wanted to set myself on fire, not my loved ones. They were in pain, and that's why I stopped cutting.

Back to square one.

Enter my room. My room is where I am most at home, yet that is not synonymous with happiness. It's the easiest setting for me--I can hide in my heavy comforter, close out the rest of the world, and bask in my pain. My fire burns alright, but my door, that gray wooden door, saves it from ever burning anyone but me. And finally, I found a safer way. A safer way to physically manifest my pain. My brain was messy, so why not make my room messy too? Whenever I felt myself going down, slowly re-entering my darkest place, I made sure my room would -slowly- became gross. Shirts threw on the ground, empty water bottles masking my floor, and school supplies covering my desk.

Where my heart is, there is no home.

Aarchi Advani.!